EMOTION, WAR AND UPRISING OF THE HUMANITY

HARSHEETH

Hi All. This is Harsheeth. Before the Introduction of story. I sincerely want to thank my mom and dad for supporting me a lot. I also want to thank all my friends who supported and helped me throughtout my ups and downs.

Contents

Preface ... *vii*

Acknowledgements ... *ix*

Prologue ... *xi*

1. Mark ... 1

2. A Prolong War ... 3

3. The Meeting ... 6

4. The Plan Fails ... 8

5. Working As A Team ... 10

6. The Diary ... 13

7. The First Time ... 19

8. The Conversation ... 21

9. The New Reign ... 29

A Note ... 33

Preface

A Warm Welcome To All The Readers. This is Harsheeth. Before going into the book, I wish to introduce myself to everyone. My name is Harsheeth and my age is 14. I am not that much experienced in writing a book. But ,still this is my first step. I already have published some of my books in online apps and website. The reason for me to write this book is the idea of the moral. I thought writing this one as my first book outside online app, so that it will give me a good confident and a small respect among the young authors. The idea of this story clicked me inorder to deliever something to the readers. Apart from a science fiction and a future based story. This story has a important message that I wished to deliever. With All My Courage I Wish This Story To Take Place In All Of Your Heart. Yours Truly Harsheeth...

Acknowledgements

Writing a book is not that much easy as I thought. This one complete book would not been completed without your help my dear friends Darshan and Sharath. You guys are the reason behind many of my success. Whenever I told that I am on a process of writing story,you always appreciated me instead of taking it as a joke. Thank you my friends.

While writing a story you should always have a person to encourage you. You are that one person who always encourages me in all my success. Thankyou Sowjanya for encouraging me a lot. I will never forget all the helps you did and all the advices you gave on writing a story.

We all need one person who motivates us. The one person who gives us strength to write a strong story. That one person who makes us believe on our own potential. One such type of person is Leela. Thank you Leela for being a very good friend.

We all need a person who can find mistakes and help us to recorrect. One such person is GuruCharan. Thank you gurucharan for helping me out in this. I really thank you for not seeing this one as a joke and instead helped me.

Atlast I need to thank many people Nitesh , Yuva , Divakar, Vishal , Rithish , Harish , Vedanth , Hari , Sakthi and Rithika for being such a good lovely friends in my life.

Prologue

Somewhere at the year 2070

Chief : Kevin, this is chief reporting. Be safe, an unknown spaceship is entering our degree of atmosphere with a brute force aiming towards our army camp.

Kevin: Ok Chief.

Kevin arranging people in order to face the spaceship with forces and troops. Nearly 24 members aiming the sky with all the weapons. Technical support team guiding them from the lab.

Chief reporting : kevin don't stay there. Tell everyone to stay out of the place. Do it now immediately.

kevin: Ok Chief.

Kevin shouting for everyone to move from the place immmediately. The army members became safe. But , thwe public over there was not in safe point . Kevin holding his breathes ran towards the people. Everyone shouted.

Suddenly the nuclears started firing here and there. A light with yellowish colour marched towards the people. There was a sudden moment of silence within the atmosphere. No one died, they all just disappered.

CHAPTER ONE

Mark

It was a beautiful seasonal spring in the city. People around the city were enjoying their lives happily. Beautiful days has beautiful moments. In the Mandal orifice auditorium, a couple was tying their knots. It was a beautiful love marriage. Around 2000 people were there. Seriously unbelievable to know that relations were still there. It was really an amazing one. The round neck ball in the front hall in which beautifully written words scripted "MARK WEDS ARNIYA."

The same day night Mark asked Arniya , Why no one came from your side of family. Arniya Replied in a dull voice saying that as she was left by her parents. No one knew the way she growed. Hearing this Mark became sad. Arniya knew that this was not the day to think about it. She went inside the kitchen and took two royal silver glass and filled it with a lovable wine and gave it to Mark. Drinking the wine and dancing on the floors , passed that night happily. After the marriage, at the year of 2045 Mark joined the army.

2045

Mark joined the army. He got a great post there. He met with a few big heads. Marik, Arlin, Enzra, and Anuriya.Each batch of 2 lakh people. Mark had 70000 people under his control . All were in the heads of four different people. Marik, Arlin, Enzra, and Anuriya were the top heads. A few fears passed by and Mark was honest hardworking person.

In a few years all of them were happy with the work of Mark and even with his character. So, Mark was given the post of general, More than 70000people with Mark in just his 5-year . This work showed his talent and hard work towards the duty. Even for the heads and team officials , it took nearly a minimum of 10 to 16 years.

But, even though in this situation he was proud of his wife. Arniya didn't work. But she was the only woman after Mark's mother who supported Mark for being who he was even in his toughest situation. Mark got married without a job or a proper degree. Everyone in his family side talked about him badly and made him feel shameless. Arniya was the only woman who believed in him. That was the thing that made him stand there. No one thought that Mark will stand in a big position with over 70000 people working under him. Mark has also given a speech in his camp, telling It's all because of my Wife. This is where the couples were standing. Showing their care, love, and affection towards each other.It was their time to discuss even further.

Their life was really going good . Until that one day. This really was meant so hard for Mark. But , this is what a destiny is all about...

CHAPTER TWO

A Prolong War

2050 was the year in which the second edition of Time machine was introduced. The time machine was a bit advanced one than the first edition. While all the higher officials and army members were on the inaugration of the second edition time machine. They got a transmitting message. The message was from 2070. Mr.Mark, the general of the Indian army started reading the message.

'This message is from 2070. We are in trouble, All the people are just getting disappered. Please help us'. We don'thave any further details about this attack.It would be better if you try anything to get us out of this.

Mr.Mark, his assistant , and two other higher officers packed all the important stuffs and troops and went to 2070. Soon, after few minutes they reached 2070. The only thing they saw there was dust. Not even a single human or animals were there at that place . After they decided to return. They heard some noise of breath and humans chattering.It was from the underground. They went to underground and there they found the Chief and Army memebers.The chief briefed about the happenings.

A Few moments later along with all the Army members and the Chief, Mr. Mark and his team returned to 2050. After reaching, with all the informations they got Mr. Mark created a small theory. Asking permission from the Chief of India Army. Mr.Mark started narrating all the happenings.

Point No 1. At The Year of 2062 There has been a meeting that took place between all The Union Leaders of the world in a big hall.

Point No 2. After This Meeting , all over the world there has been a suspicious thing that has taken place

Point No 3. The First Suspcious thing is over the eight years many childrens have died before the age of 15. The fact is that all the childrens have not died naturally but some drastic incident has taken place.

Point No 4. After This 8 years now some people have been disappered and the count of people who got disappeared is 7 cr.

Point No 5. According to my theory. If we know what had hapened on the meeting that took place at the big hall will give us any clues for the further leads of this tragedy that's being taken place.

Point No 6. We also have a problem. None of us have the access to enter that big hall on that day and though trying to spy them is really tough. As one of the high quality security check is present at that place.

So, here by I finish my theory and All I need is an idea. If anyone has any idea or opposite theory regarding this can kindly raise your hands.

Batch No 231 (Head): I guess it would be better if we wait and take a final decision

Special Batch (Captain): How do you expect us to wait. Are you going crazy.

People from Batch 231 and special batch starting a quarrel between each others. The auditorium getting a bit controversial and suddenly the Chief starts speaking.

Chief: Silence. Please do not fight here. This is not where we should waste our energy. Please do maintain silence. We would wait for sometime , to create a perfect plan. It doesn't matter how much time we are planning and executive. But , remember each time , we should plan perfectly. Now dismiss.

After finishing the meeting. There was a small round table conference among the chief , the general and two other higher officials.

Chief: The theory was perfect. But , definetly its tough for us to cope up with it. But , I know one thing regarding that meeting. The meeting was officially announced by the Union Head Mr. Winset Richard.

After finshing this conversation, all of them went to their respective rooms. Mark Started thinking about this deeply and finally came with an imaginary line up.

CHAPTER THREE

The Meeting

In The big hall, 2062 (According To Mark's Assumption)
Winset Richard(The Head Of Union Leaders Of The World):

A Warm welcome to one and all present here. I am the head of the union Mr.Winset Richard. I have gathered all of you here for this meeting for talking about a big problem. As we checked with an advanced device named morali. A Device used for the checking the expectancy. We came to know that by the year 2074 the earth will be destroyed into by shrinkage. The reason why I am talking here is that we have found a new planet. The planet has all the sufficients needs like our earth. Its really hard to leave our mother Earth. But what can we do. We have come to the end of this beautiful world. But to say this is not the real problem. The real difficulty is that only 700000 billion people can live there. But in our world there are more people.

So , what we are we going to do.

We hereby , will start creating new agent robots. All this robots will be given specific names. We are going to allot each robots for each babies that are going to be born after this year. We will hereby fix a death date for the babies. When the baby reaches that particular age that baby will be killed by our agent robots. You may ask How are you going to make the parents accept. We are going to lie.

Even atlast if we lack in the increase of number. Plan B is to select each badass person from every street of the country. At one auspicious day we will launch a new siringe of Auto oxygenated pylancinite acid which would easily kill the people. This siringe will be launched according to the atmosphere degrees and arrangements. From our Satelite Winset Development the siringe will be sent..

So , by this our population also reduces and all of us can live the life we want till our death date, instead of sacrificing our lifes for the new generation.

All Of Us Know That Humanity had died many years ago and no longer this will be a sin for us. In the new planet all the countires will be united to form a single country.One Democracy , One Country , One Reign and One Law. Thank you All.

Some random man shouting from the back: As of do you think you are the king. You are just a bastard. How All of you are sitting silently. We first have to kill this Bastard.

Even after hearing this all were maintaining silence. Mr. Winset slowly walked out of the hall. Calling his PA , Winset ordered to kill that bastard who shouted inside the hall..

CHAPTER FOUR

The Plan Fails

2050

When Mark was getting ready for another meeting. He recieved a call.

Stranger speaking: Hello Mark. Can you please find an answer for me. It is a simple question. Who am I ?. Can you answer this question Mark. You can't because you don't know anything about me and will not. I am telling you one thing. There is no life for some people after 2070. So, you just say everyone to be happy till 2070 and don't waste your time by searching me. Bye.

Mark had a tracing machine. When using the tracing machine, Mark came to know that the call was from various timeline with various places. In the starting of the call, it showed 2042, then it showed 2069 and atlast it showed 2054. So the fact is that ,there is no use in tracing.

After a few minutes. Mark went to the conference. There the chief came. He asked for clues. Mark replied with a delegant smile in his face saying, Yes Sir we have got two clues. First clue is, This is not an alien attack or a robot attack. It is a human all behind this. The second clue is he wants to rule the world without some specific humans and We don't know the reason behind it.

Chief : I guess the Second clue is of no use, gentleman.

Mark: No sir. If he wants to rule.

Point one. We have time machine, he has to be at any one of the future timeline after 2070. Because he can't rule before 2069.

Point two. First he will come to 2042 and kill Albert. Then he can take control of everything he wants even if we are alive in this timeline or any other timeline . Because the first time machine was released at 2042 by Albert. Now the second edition also by Albert. If he kills Albert, then definetly we won't have time machine.

Chief: So what we are going to do

Mark: Sir, his next target will be 2042. So we have to find him at 2042

Chief: Very good . You go with higher officers to 2042.

The conference ends with a quite satisfaction. Soon After discussing about this, eight of the higher officers including Mark started packing their troops and went to 2042. But this is were Mark understood the real issue of this problem . He was just stunned of what he saw in the big screen of New York. A message was written to Mark.

Mr.Albert died. So, you can't go back to 2050 as your timemachine is now vanished. You also don't have resources to make a time machine. Now You are struck in 2042. Good Bye.

CHAPTER FIVE

Working As A Team

Mr.Albert has once shared a secret with Mark and it striked Mr.Mark at that moment. It was nothing but at 2045 for the first time, time machine was introduced and it was said that Mr.Albert found the resources. But the real thing is it was not Albert who found the resource. It was his friend who was an archaeologist found the resource in a place at 2042. He gave it to Mr.Albert. This information was told to Mark on his marriage by Albert. So, maybe the resource was already in underground. So, if mark could dig the right place, they would be able to find it and do a time machine and go back to 2050.

He was not sure about that idea. So, they were thinking about an other idea. As no other ideas stuck in their head. They thought of moving on with this idea.

Mr.Mark though of askng help to another scientist named Arman. When Mark along with the others went to Arman's lab. They came to know that Arman was not there and instead his assistand was present there.

Richard : Hi, I am Richard. Do you want any help. I am Scientist Mr. Arman's assistant.

Mark : Hi , I am Mark. I am an archaeologist. Yes I want an help, I forgot to bring my tools in a hurry. Could you please give me any tool for digging the ground.

Richard : Yes, sir for sure I can help you. But the thing is you look like an army person and all of you.

Mark : This is new army haircut(giggled mark without a satisfaction).

Richard : Ohh. Just 2 mins sir, I will bring my digger.

Then as soon as possible Mr. Richard helped them and they started digging the ground. They first checked the place and it was the right place. They started digging as possible as they worked. They couldn't find the resources.

Mr. Richard told: When you go more deeper today itself it will be not good for your health even if you were safety. So,they all started taking rest there itself.

After some time, Richard came and asked about few informations. The first question was , where was their home located.

Mark replied saying our home is too far. Without a minute of hesitation , Richard asked them to stay in his house and treated them as a friend and served them very well. Soon they went to sleep.

While all of them were sitting in the main hall. Mark asked Richard about the scars he had on his neck and face. But Richard didn't reply for it. By this the night went away.

Two Days Later

It was the Third day morning and still they were digging. They dig 50,653ft deep. It was more deep enough. But , they didn't find the resource. At last at the third day morning 10:30 they found the resource. They asked

Richard for help to do the time machine. But for their surprise, they came to know that Richard was so intelligent enough for making a time machine.

Richard told: I have a time machine in my lab. But it is not working. It may need a better resource. Maybe you might help me. We can repair it in a few days.

After working very hard for 2 weeks.They inserted that resource in the time machine and it worked successfully. Mark thanked Richard for helping him a lot. Soon , after that they reached 2050 safely. After reaching only Mark realised that While they were working on the machine, he would have found a diary written by Richard's son. Unfortunately it was in Mark's bag. As they were sitting simply. He opened and read the first line. After reading that he was very curious of reading the diary...

CHAPTER SIX

The Diary

Hi , Dear Diary.

This is Winset Richard. I am writing this Diary To open up all the worries I have. Because I have no one to say all this. My father is there, but he is already broken. When I was 7 years old , the life was really beautiful.

My Father Richard , My Mom Sinia and my elder sister Salia Winset, all of us together were a wonderful family. My father was not an Indian. But , once when he came India he fell in love with my mom and married her. They were in love for 6 years and many times my father narrated me their love story. From the way they met, the conversations , the arguements and atlast the marriage. This is how our life was.

Then My Father was a general in the army and my mom was a housewife. Even thenThe days were very happy. All the nights of the summer , spring and the cold winter. Everything was very good. Years passed then very quickly. We all had a lovely pet named Tinko who was always with us. Tinko was very well trained dog as it was on traing for two years in the camp at that time. Tinko was so fit enough and because of him , I was also fit. Because , I was the one who used to play and go on for walking with Tinko.

As we all have come across with a quote " Life doesnt always go the way we expect". That is where it all started. I thought Life was way too easy to live on until and unless that seven days nightmare came upon.

On A Fine Wednesday Night. My father rushed to our home with blood stains in his general shirt and sweat over all his body and deep breathes that had a silence and a long way in it. He told there took place a big mistake and his own army members are now against him . He told living a life here would not be nice.

We packed all the important thing in a hurry. As a 7 year old boy I stood there blinking my eyes not knowing what was happening. When we packed everything and hurried towards the back door. Suddenly three mens entered inside and locked us apart. There started that seven days nightmare.

DAY 1

On The first day. We didn't even get a small piece of bread to eat. We were left hungry . All we had was plenty of water. Some people used to enter inside our house. They used to beat my father and pull him sliding inside a room. They used to start shouting at him and all I used to hear from outside is the word " Speak the Truth".

I still remember that I used to ask all the people over there What's happening with a little baby face not knowing that our family is undergoing a torture were the whole humanity died. I used to sit next to my sister and I ask her what is happening and all she does is keeps my head in her chest making me lie on her and her tears would drop on my backbone.

In The night. I am the only one who slept in my family. My father was sitting staright thinking of How to save us. My mom was lying down crying and the sister who was sitting staright making me lie on her lap and holding tears in her eyes, singing songs for me with that weaken feeble voice.

DAY 2

It was the second day. This day I would never forget in my life. The pain of this day is like a fire that can never be exhausted. It will stay in my heart throught my life time. My father came up with a plan of escaping. He narrated the way we were going to escape to my sister and mom.

Everything was going as per our plan. It was in the night we thought of escaping, So , around at 7PM we slowly jumped down from the attic. One of the guard saw us. My mother and my sister's face suddenly turned life a darken mid forest flowers not able to blossom properly(Indirectly meaning the way of sorrow). The guard's name was Adam. He was not a guard but a gof for us. He helped us there. We thought we were on a right track. So , now First my father lifted my sister and threw her the other side of the yard.

Like this for the second time I was lifted and transfered to the other side of the yard. He clearly mentioned both of us never to wait for them, instead run away as far as we can.

When it was time for both my mom and dad to come. They were catched up by then. After running a few miles far. Both of us got caught by them. All I along with my sister thought was just we didn't finish the plan successfully. But when we reached the home. That's were still my heart ache.

My father was sitting like a statue in the corner with tears half hold in his eyes and the other half dried up in his skin. I still remember the words I heard in my ears from the guards. Take a nude video of that lady and throw her away somewhere.

Just for a moment not knowing the full meaning of what they meant , myself a seven year old boy was sitting for two days hoping that I would see my mother soon.

A 13 year old girl who was mentally suffocating from all this in fears and tears was still holding me lying in her chest and that's were our love lied and their humanity died.

DAY 3,4

These two days were somewhat fine. We were not physically harmed. But , my sister and my father were mentally harmed. I asked my sister repeatedly about the happenings. She never replied. She just was keep on crying until her face was fully dried up with the tears. I missed those days when I used to play so happily in the yards along with my dog and my sister.

I was hoping for the days to become normal. Where I would go to school and meet my friends. Study interesting things. Return back home. Eat delicious snacks and start playing with my dog. Again in the evening wait for my sister's van. The way I used to hug her when she gets down from her van. The cute little fight between us and so on.

I missed all those beautiful days. These two days went in hoping that something would change. Then the next day came

DAY 5, 6

Even at these two days we were Hoping that all this would end soon and we will all live back normally. Still we were drinking only plenty of water.

That is when I came to know what was it all about when the other two officials were talking. The army that my father was working was doing something illegally. Knowing the cause of it, my father has stood against them in saving many lakhs people out of this cruel plan by the army.

Knowing this he is now suffering from this problem. Withought knowing this myself and my sister were suffering these days.

But even at that time and now I know that my father is a real hero. He was never at a wrong situation or side in his whole time and still now I don't understand why good people's end up badly , I strongly mean it.

These two days went like this. Like a slow moving snail. In the end of the day 6 we got something to eat. That time I didn't realise anything and enjoyed that food. But , then after that seven days, I understood it was my own dog Tinko which was served to us.

DAY 7

I thought that all of this was over by now and that's when I came to know that this day is most tragedic day among the all seven days.

One big person came and kneeled down in front of me and said. If you want you can close your eyes my dear little boy. Because now your lovable sister is going to suffer. Do you know why I am leaving your father and you as it is. Once your father told me that like him , he would make you stand as a honest officer. I wish to see him suffer in pain while raising you from now.

I didn't what was that man was all about. Few days ago only my heart ached. Now my whole body was burning. The way I cried, the pain. This one will never leave my life. I am still struggling to sleep in the nights. I am still dreaming about that day as a nightmare.

With tears filled in my eyes. Crying and shouting until my voice breaks, I saw my sister being raped. A just small 13 years old caring sister who is being raped in front of his own brother. I could still imagine that day in my eyes.

After this incident , two years later my sister herself suicided and died. Now my thought is not only to overcome from this situation. Also to overcome from the belief that still humanity is alive. Now I decided perfectly. I will create a Union were all the ones are the ones who had lost belief in humanity.

I will create a world with One Democracy , One Reign and One law.

CHAPTER SEVEN

The First Time

Reading the diary I came to know that I found the man behind all this. I thought this wouldn't end this soon by a small diary written by a boy. But , still its good that this one ends. I didn't wish to tell about this to anyone. Because, I really felt the pain. All I needed now is to meet Myr. Winset Richard and clarify some of my doubts. So , dealed this one differently. I went to the Chief's room and had a conversation with him.

Mark : Chief , I guess the best idea is to meet him personally and catch him. I have an idea and all I need is your permission. First of all I am going to challenge him to come one by one with the help of the big screen. One more thing I really don't want anyone for backup. I wish to deal this one myself and please do trust me.

Chief: Ok. I am trusting you general Mark. But , please don't break my trust.

Mark: Sure Chief.

I walked out of the room with a joy in my face. After getting permission from the chief. I started delievering the words in the big screen.

" To Mr. Stranger. I Now knew All About You. All I need is Coversation with you. I f you guts call Me"

As I expected , I got a call. But this was not a call by Richard. Instead I got this call from some random robotic voice demanding me to come to one place. I din't expect directly Richard would wish us to see face to face. But , still what I wished has taken place. I didn't take any weapone or any sort of fear inside me. With full hopes and guts that this would end properly I went to that place.

That is where for the first time I met Mr.Winset Richard(The Head Of The Union Leaders Of 2070). It was really so dark and thrill chilling place all around with glasses and advanced and royal tech structures. Soon our conversation began...

CHAPTER EIGHT

The Conversation

Winset: Hi Mark. Nice to Meet You. Seems like you wanted to talk with me.

Mark: Yeah Mr. Unknown. But I never thought you would directly arrange this session.

Winset: Ohh , really. What's the matter bold man.

Mark: Actually you think I don't know anything about you. But , I do Mr. Winset Richard. Second time when I time travelled to 2042. We got stuck. That's when a gentleman helped us. His name was Richard. Probably I guess you know who he is. Your father only helped us and saved us. Then the second fact is that. I had a diary that was written by a small boy named Winset Richard. By these words I guess you understood what I am trying to deliever here. Now I am not here to harm you by any chance Winset. I am here to clarify two doubts.

1) I accept that the tragedy that took place in your life is a very harmful one. But what's the reason for making people dissappear for that. What did those 7 crore people do in you life.

2) What did the small new born babies did. You are so angry on humanity. Where was your humanity in these things. Do you think that small babies are the scapegoats for your anger, Whatever had happened. The path you have

taken is wrong. I need a proper justification for this.

Winset: Young Gentlemen. What you said is correct according to your perspective. But do you wanna know all the truth behind this drama. Don't feel too confused. Listen to my words from your bottom of the heart deeply.

You are not here because you wanted to meet me. You are here because I wanted to meet you. Do you know, On that seven day nightmare I saw one guard who was suffering along with us. He was not happy in doing that sin. That one guard helped our family throughout our seven day tragedy. Do you know who is that guard. Your Beloved father Adam Mark.

I thought that he would definetly raise you in a good way in this cruel world. So , I choosed you in this. The reason you came to know this tragedy is by me. The reason you went to 2042 was a plan made by me. The reason my father came and spoke with you was my plan and atlast now you are standing opposite to me and this is also a plan that was executed by me perfectly..

What's this all about. You think the people who were missing are somewhere transmitted. No , they are all dead. The fact is that they are all the people who were reasons behind the sufferings of many families like mine. You may ask what about the babies. The babies aren't dead. They are just being raised by robots with good human qualities as I thought that their father's wouldn't raise them in a proper way . They would definetly have raised them in a badass way.

Humanity is not destroyed as you said. It is being destroyed by some people. Humanity is not only helping someone when they are in need. Humanity is when you understand all people living in this world are just like you and seeing everyone equally and one among you.

I would die in 2 hours. You are now in a coma. All this has not taken place. Only the disappearing of some peoples and my tragedy is true. When you wake up from this coma. You will become the president of this new country. You are going to take this process of One Democracy , One Reign and One Humanity. One more thing, when you wake up your wife will be next to you.

I also wanted to share you some things. Do you know the reason behind why did my family suffer? or Do you know what actually happened on the meeting?. Just listen. I will narrate the truth.

In 2034

Two countries were the major reasons for the world war 3. In that two countries , my father was the general of one country. Our country was in a situation to raise a nuclear threat. If that nuclear was lauched at that time, definetly nearly including the supporting countries of the opposition about 6 crore people would have died and in that probably 3.6 would have been innocent people. To stop this threat only my father was struggling. In one point of situation my father came to know that his words will no longer have impact.

My Father was the general at that time and he had the access to the room where that nuclear was located. The fact is that as the technology was updated, the nuclear now had fixed timing. All it does is when it reaches the number zero , wherever it is placed on there it will blast. My father first taught of changing the destination. But he was not handling that system and definetly he could not do that.

My father knew that our family would suffer. But , never he expected that much cruelity. He even taught that there would be some people to help him there. But no one was there. Now what he did was , instead of misplacing the nuclear.

My father brilliantly used a time machine and sended that nuclear to 1860. You may ask How did my father have a time machine at 2030 , if the first time machine was built in 2045. Apart from a general my father was a scientist. Before Albert found time machine, my father found. It was not officially announced because in 2030 they taught time machines would be used for wrong things.

That's where everyone in the camp were confused. How could a nuclear get dissappeared. When hearing this only I understood that this was the reason behind the work " Speak The Truth" in the interrogation room. The real problem is , the army people were scared because they taught now the opposing country would raise a nuclear.

That was the reason behind our suffering. But atlast the opposing country came up with white flag for piece. We were not given any justice or compensation for that. You may again have a doubt. If we had time machine. Why didn't we use it. Once my father told this,

" If one thing is meant to happen in life. It will happen. Changing that it not what life is. Even now I am happy that my wife and my daughter were very bold enough to die and this death is what bravery. If I had changed this, that doesn't mean the people who made us suffer will change. But now somewhere in their heart they will feel our pain and understand their mistake. So , let it be."

This one quote from my father is enough for me to have a satisfaction that My Father Is A Real Hero..

After telling this Winset Cries. Not knowing what's actually happening. Is this all believable, Mark stands like a statue. After a few moments of silence Winset again continues speaking. Now its time for explaining what actually happened on the meeting

In The Big Hall , 2062.

Winset Richard(TheHead Of Union Leaders Of The World):

A Warm welcome to one and all present here. As you all know I am the head of the union Mr.Winset Richard, This is my responsibility. The reasom I have gathered all of you here for this meeting is to talk about a big problem. As we checked with our advance device morali. A Device used for the checking the expectancy. We came to know that by the year 2074 the earth will be destroyed by shrinkage. The reason why I am talking here is that we have found a new planet. The planet has all the sufficient needs like our earth. Its really hard to leave our mother Earth. But what can we do. We have come to the end of this beautiful world. But to say the truth, this is not the real problem. The real difficulty is that only 700000 billion people can live there. But in our world there are more people.

So , what we are we going to do.

We hereby , will start creating new agent robots. All this robots will be given specific names. We are going to allot each robots for each babies that are going to be born after this year. We will hereby fix a death date for the babie's fathers. When the baby reaches that particular age that particular babies father will be killed by our agent robots.

You may ask How can we kill their father. For that only we are gonna choose people like robbers, criminals , and badass people who doesn't deserve to live in this world. I know this is a sin and definetly their wives would also suffer. But we are going to do all this with some people's acceptance only. Even a smuggler or a criminal will be ready to sacrifice his life for his baby. That is the power of a Father. Let them also vanish away their sins and let the new planet begin with cleanliness. We need that robots to take care like the fathers.

Soon more than we expected , many people were ready to sacrifice their lives. Including some retired and old age people.

Plan B is to select each person from every street of the country. At one day we will launch a new siringe of Auto oxygenated pylancinite acid which would easily kill the people. This siringe will be launched according to the atmosphere degrees and arrangements. From our Satelite Winset Development the siringe will be sent..

So , if needed we will also sacrifice our lifes for the new generation. This is definetly good and pretty much understandable.

still can't believe this. Here some words from the background. Those are the words from the letters that were wriiten by great fathers who sacrificed their lifes for their sons and daughters.

An Imaginary Voice

Letter 1

Hey Son , This is your father. I know that you think your father as a hero. But, I am not a hero like you think. I am criminal who has killed nearly 12 people for money and has kidnapped many people in my life. But , do you know one thing. On April 4 , when I recieved you in my hands for the first time. The mistakes I did in my whole life time flashed infornt of me. That's when I changed. Now because of me many people are living. You were the one who gave me a second chance. Now I think this sacrifice is nothing infront of the mistakes I did. Just remember never be a bad person in life. Concentrate on your studies. Because , education is one of the best weapons. I love you so much my dear son. When you read this letter I won't be alive. But , still I guess I will be alive in your heart.

Letter 2

My dear Saariya , This is your father. You are my whole world. You may think now I am also leaving you. Don't worry. Do you know why your mother left me. The father you see was not the husband your mother saw. Because , I was a drug dealer. One time because of me six teenage boys and three girls consumed drugs and were dies. That is why your mother left me. But , When the first time after returning from the jail , I came to know that your mother left. But she left you for me to understand the life. The moment I saw you , that three girls who died infront of me came to my rememberance. Your father actually dies many years ago. Now he is really sacrificing his life and its all for you. Be a brave and good girl. Love you dear.

Like this there are many people all around the world. This is what this was all about. But, atlast this what I wanted to share with you. The first page of a diary from a girl named Aniya. Just listen and feel the pain.

From The Diary

Page 1

Hi dear diary. My name is Aniya. My age is 16 currently. Since 5 years old I was being abused by some criminals. There was one particular man who saved me. His name was Winset. I am really grateful. Till that moment I thought there was no hope in my life. Winset himself raised me in his lab. He never showed me to anyone else. Literally for two moths it was hard for me to believe him. But , on midnight of a fine wednesday I heard someone crying. So , out from my bed I came and saw. Sitting in the couch like a small kid Winset was crying. I went near him and asked what happened. He didn't narrate anything. But , instead he said one word and that word is Still in my heart. " You Look Like My Sister".

I saw a deep feelings through his eyes. A feeling of missing someone loads. Winset was the one who made me understand the true feeling of love. Love is not something between two people around with romantic scenaries. Love is a beautiful word which is expressed for showing our care and affection towards someone. Love is a words which indirectly depicts that I am there for you. Winset have only interacted with me sometimes. But each time he made me feel the world in a good way.

I have never seen my parents or anyone who is related to me after that incident. But I can happily and proudly see Winset has my father. Actually he really cared me in that way. In this whole diary, apart fom my self pain and struggles. I am going to speak about the man behind my happiness....

The Imaginary Voice Slowly Starts To Vanish.

Richard Speaks

This is the sole reason for my sacrifice. I don't know from where this path started and where its now going to end. But , I am damn sure that I have lived a life where I have gained place in many people's heart. I hope you would understand everything. Lead the new part of life. You too live a life that you would be appreciated for. Let the Earth's Prosper Stand Within.

FEW DAYS LATER

As The New President Of The Country. Myself Mark, Son of Adam Mark Hereby Announce the new policy of One Democracy , One Reign , One Law and One Humanity.....

CHAPTER NINE

The New Reign

New Constitutional Laws

1: As all The Countries Are United. No One Has The Rights To Start A War.

2: All Are Equal Among The Law. The One Who Violates Will Be Punished Very Severely. No Matter from which Country he was.

3: The Head Of All The Army Will Hereafter Be Lead By Retired Honest Officials

4:There will be only three main goverments. No politicians.

5: Everyone in the country has to do all the works. No one has the permenant jobs than officials.

6:The Retired officers can order and rule according to their age.

7: Everybody are brothers and sisters. No one has the rights to destroy others life.

8: There is only one Oath and One National anthem for the country.

9: The national anthem is for 12 minutes.

10: Everyday morning at 10:00 , all peoples should walk out from their home or offices and stand in the street for the National anthem.

11: There will be no police. People who stay near has to help others if any need. If they fail to save or help the other person , they will be punished.

12: All The brands of electronics and mechanics are available to all the people.

13: All The works should be till 9PM only , except jobs like banks.etc.

14: Everyone will have to use the emergency device if any problem for them or to someone else.

15: One Democracy, One Reign , One Humanity.

After this New Rules were added to the Law Book. The new life Began. It was really a great success than expected.

Few Days Later

It was fine quite summer evening. The first week in the new planet. The new planet was also named Earth according to the people as they completely believed that Earth is what their mother land name is. All the people over different countries are now living in a single land. The mind blowing and the most happiest thing is that Out of religion , caste , creed, colour , language, racism and many number of problems. Now people are living among each other. In this itself a small piece of Humanity is included.

Every pleasent morning people would go for work. Sharp at 10 AM all of them would come and stand in the streets of new national anthem. Nobody used to work after 9PM. People who believed in good and humanity thought this was the right thing. Life here started going good.

The Funeral

It was the funeral of Winset Richard. Many people attended the funeral. The fact that admired me personally was , Really Winset has gained a good respect among people. He had lived such a worthy life like a legend. I am really happy for that. Soon after few minutes everyone started giving speech regarding Winset. But , I was waiting for one person to give the speech. His Sister.

Arniya: A Warm welcome to one and all present here. I am Arniya , sister of Winset Richard. Winset was such a lovely brother. From a seven years little boy who not knowing what happened in some tragic situation who lied in my chest to now creating such a big and good revolution among people, Winset has really grown. Not only in this lifetime , In all my lifetime I wish Winset to be my brother. If I speak more than this definetly I would cry. But, I don't want to cry. Because once Winset told me this

" You should not cry even on my funeral. Because , from that day I am sure about one thing. I never want to see my sister cry anymore in the life. Please don't cry. If you cry surely my soul will not rest in peace."

After hearing the speech , I started crying. Now it was my turn. I walked on the stairs and slowly reached towards the stage. I was standing with my legs slightly shaking in nervousness. But , holding my legs steadily, I started speaking. All I spoke about was from the diary I wrote after becoming the president. A small note for Winset Richard.

Note(From The Diary Of Mark)

Winset, I know that you are not in this world anymore. But , I know that you could see all the happenings. I still can't believe some things and am not sure about all. But , one thing is sure in my mind. Life may be not in the way as we think. But a small piece of respect and a way of living is what everyone needs.

As you wished this world will change. Humanity will raise. Everyone humans have good in them and some show them and the rest doesn't. But as you said feeling others life and cosidering everyone you see as a person among you

, creates a perfect man.

I really want to thank you Winset for making me realize some good things in life. Many times in my life I have thought bad about my father. But , you made me realize how heroic was my father in living such a lovely life. I will definetly save your hopes and develop the country.

A Note

Hi All. This is a note that I wished to deliever to you readers as an Author. The main reason and idea of this story is to convey the importance of Humanity. Humanity is always not among the one in world. It is among people. Try to open up the good side from your heart. You may think this world is cruel or fake. You may think why should I be good. You may think of being a heartless man or woman. But remember one thing. the one's who are meant to stay with you will definetly stay with you. So , it doesn't mean being heartless is the best attitude. First priority is your happiness and the second prority is making happy people who make you happy. The third priority is when you realize everyone are like you and cosider them one among you, even if they hurt you.

Thank You

A Note and A Story By Harsheeth